HOLY SQUAWKAMOLE!

LITTLE RED HEN MAKES GUACAMOLE

retold by Susan Wood   illustrated by Laura González

STERLING CHILDREN'S BOOKS
New York

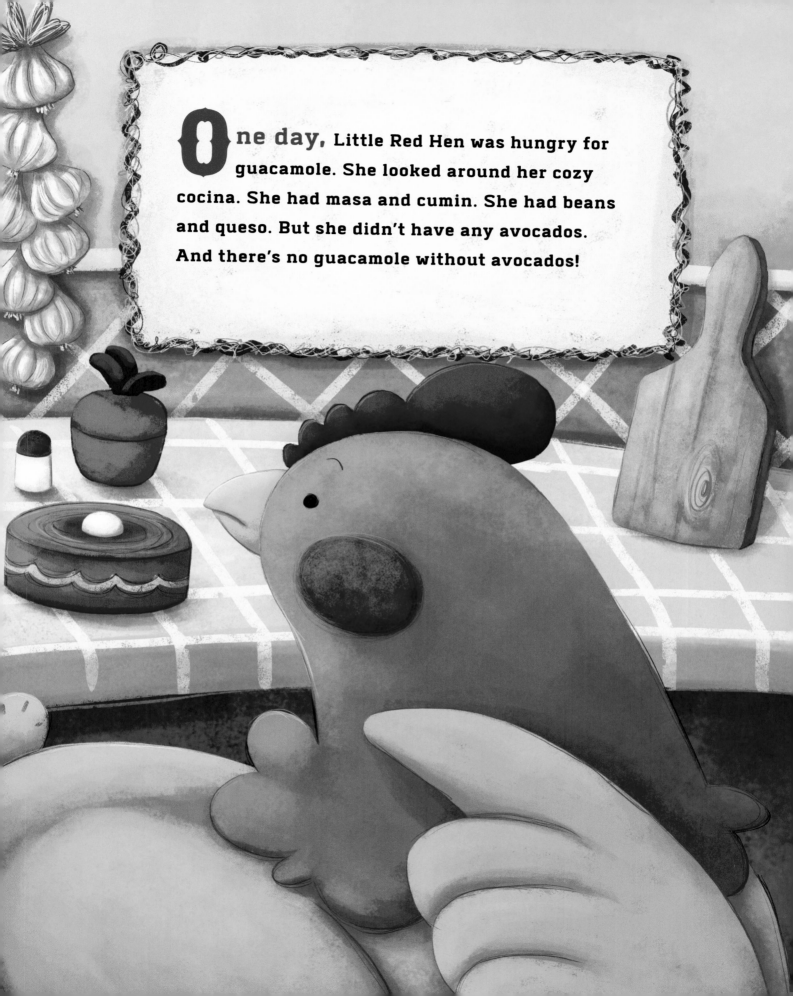

One day, Little Red Hen was hungry for guacamole. She looked around her cozy cocina. She had masa and cumin. She had beans and queso. But she didn't have any avocados. And there's no guacamole without avocados!

So Little Red Hen trotted to the avocado grove.

"HOLY SQUAWKamoLe!" she clucked.

"That's a tall tree! Coati, will you help
me gather avocados for my guacamole?"

"I'm hanging out. But I'll help eat it when it's done, gallinita roja. Nothing beats a tasty guacamole."

"Then I'll gather the avocados myself," said Little Red Hen.
And she did.

Now Little Red Hen had her avocados, but she needed tomatoes. There's no guacamole without tomatoes! So Little Red Hen trotted to the vegetable garden.

"HOLY SQUAWKAMOLE!" she clucked.

"Those tomato vines are tangly! Snake, will you help me pluck tomatoes for my guacamole?"

"Not I," hissed Snake.

"I'm all tied up. But I'll help eat it when it's done, gallinita roja. Nothing beats a tasty guacamole."

"Then I'll pluck the tomatoes myself," said Little Red Hen.

And she did.

Now Little Red Hen had her avocados and tomatoes, but she needed onions. There's no guacamole without onions! So Little Red Hen trotted to the onion patch.

"HOLY SQUAWKAMOLE!" she clucked.

"Those onions are buried so deep! Armadillo, will you help me dig onions for my guacamole?"

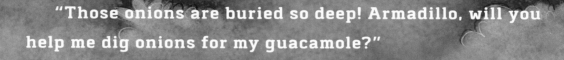

"Not I," grunted Armadillo.

"I gotta jump. But I'll help eat it when it's done, gallinita roja. Nothing beats a tasty guacamole."

"Then I'll dig the onions myself," said Little Red Hen. And she did.

Now Little Red Hen had her avocados, tomatoes, and onions, but she needed cilantro. There's no guacamole without cilantro!

So Little Red Hen trotted to the herb garden.

"HOLY SQUAWKAMOLE!" she clucked.

"That cilantro is bushy! Iguana, will you help me snip cilantro for my guacamole?"

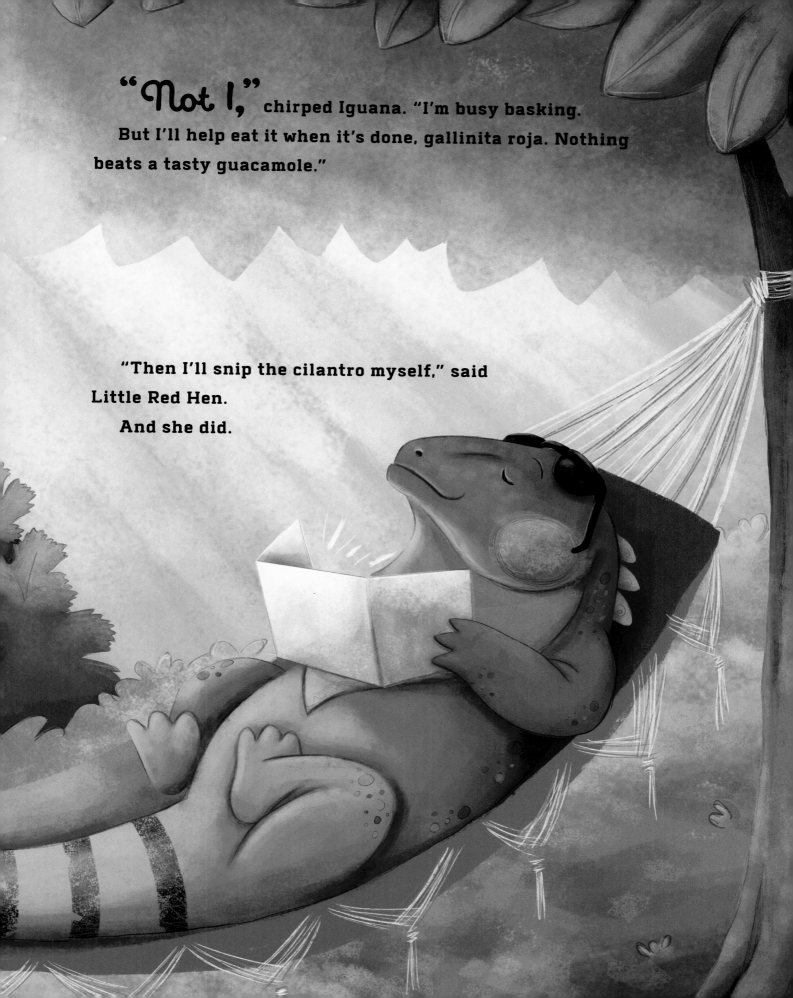

"**Not I,**" chirped Iguana. "I'm busy basking. But I'll help eat it when it's done, gallinita roja. Nothing beats a tasty guacamole."

"Then I'll snip the cilantro myself," said Little Red Hen.
And she did.

Now Little Red Hen had her avocados, tomatoes, onions, and cilantro, and she needed to mash and mix them. There's no guacamole without mashing and mixing!

So Little Red Hen trotted back to her casa.

"HOLY SQUAWKAMOLE!"

she clucked.

"This molcajete is a lot of work!
Who will help me mash and mix?"

"But we'll help eat it when it's done, gallinita roja," they said together. "Nothing beats a tasty guacamole."

"Then I'll mash and mix myself," said Little Red Hen.

And she did.

Then she added
something special.

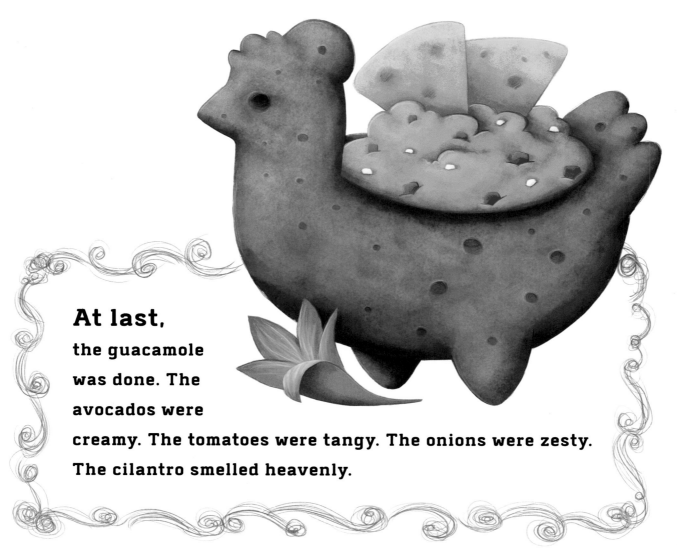

At last,
the guacamole
was done. The
avocados were
creamy. The tomatoes were tangy. The onions were zesty.
The cilantro smelled heavenly.

"I will!"
snorted Coati.

"I will!"
hissed Snake.

"I will!"
chirped Iguana.

"I will!"
grunted Armadillo.

"Nothing beats a tasty guacamole!"
they said together.

Coati tucked it into a taco. Snake scooped it with a tortilla. Armadillo rolled it into a burrito. Iguana slurped it straight.

"Mmmm,"
they all said.

Suddenly, they stopped chewing.

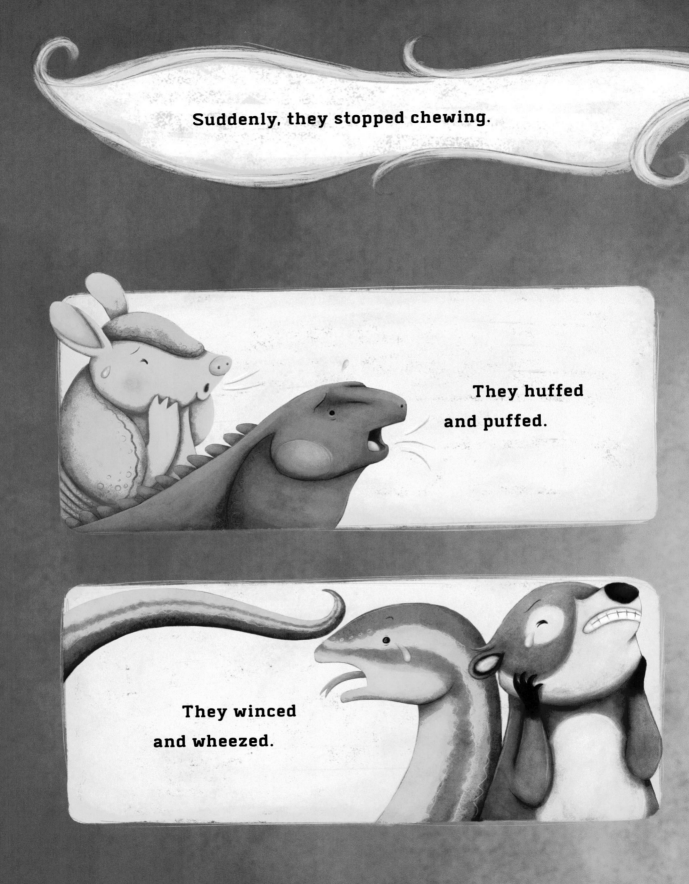

They huffed
and puffed.

They winced
and wheezed.

They sweated and slobbered.

"HOLY SQUAWKAMOLE!"

they all hollered.

Little Red Hen smiled.
"Nothing beats a tasty
guacamole!" she clucked.

And together they ate every spicy bit.

THE STORY OF
GUACAMOLE

Guacamole is a yummy blend of mashed avocado, vegetables, and seasonings. Although most people think of it as a dip, it's actually a sauce—a sauce that's hundreds of years old!

It's believed that the Aztecs of Mexico first made ahuacamolli, or "avocado sauce," in the 1300s. When Spanish explorers came to Mexico in the 1500s, they found the Aztecs using a stone mortar and pestle, or molcajete, to mash up ripe avocados with a variety of tomatoes, onions, hot peppers, and cilantro. The Spaniards loved the delicious sauce and brought it back with them to Europe. Over time, the name changed from ahuacamolli to "guacamole."

Though guacamole was first mashed and mixed in Mexico, today the sauce is made and enjoyed all over the world. Most traditional recipes call for the same ingredients the Aztecs used. But there's really only one required ingredient—there's no guacamole without avocado!

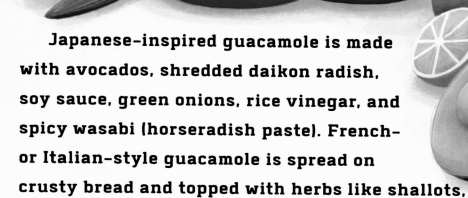

Japanese-inspired guacamole is made with avocados, shredded daikon radish, soy sauce, green onions, rice vinegar, and spicy wasabi (horseradish paste). French- or Italian-style guacamole is spread on crusty bread and topped with herbs like shallots, tarragon, basil, and garlic. Caribbean-influenced guacamole uses fresh mango, papaya, pineapple, and even pomegranate seeds to give it a fruity flair. In America, the sauce is typically served as a dip with tortilla chips at parties and celebrations and as a tasty snack.

Guacamole is so beloved in America, in fact, that it even has its own holiday. September 16 is National Guacamole Day (as well as Mexican Independence Day). Guacamole's so delicious, though, that we eat it all year round—because nothing beats a tasty guacamole!

HOLY SQUAWKAMOLE GUACAMOLE

Want to make your own guacamole? Here's la gallinita roja's recipe.

INGREDIENTS

2 large ripe avocados

1–2 small red tomatoes, chopped (chop
  these items carefully
or ask a grown-up for help)

1 small white onion, chopped

chopped cilantro leaves

½ teaspoon salt (2.85 grams)

(OPTIONAL) 1 jalapeño pepper,
  finely diced with seeds removed
  (wear gloves while preparing or wash
  your hands well after handling)

CHILI PEPPER OPTIONAL!

DIRECTIONS

1. Carefully cut the avocado lengthwise down the center around the seed (or ask a grown-up for help). Twist the two halves apart. One half will contain the large seed; remove it by sliding a spoon between the seed and the green fruit inside the skin. With the spoon, scoop the fruit out of the skin and into a bowl. Cut, seed, and scoop the other avocado too.

2. Use a fork to mash the avocado fruit in the bowl. Don't mash too much—it's okay if it's chunky!

3. Add the tomato, onion, and cilantro to taste (that means add however much *you* like!), plus the salt and (OPTIONAL) jalapeño pepper.

4. Mix it all up with the fork.

HOLY SQUAWKAMOLE! YOU JUST MADE YOUR OWN GUACAMOLE!

HELPFUL HINTS

- To tell if an avocado is ripe, give it a gentle squeeze—if it's firm but just a little soft, it's ready. Too hard means it's not ripe yet; too squishy means it's overripe.

- Avocado out of its peel turns brown the longer it's exposed to air. Adding a ½ tablespoon of lemon or lime juice to your guacamole will help it stay beautifully green. When storing leftover guacamole, press plastic wrap to the surface of the guacamole to keep air out.

- Add your own special ingredients—traditional Mexican flavors like cumin, garlic, or some salsa, or get creative with fruit, veggies, and other spices.

- Tuck your guacamole into a taco, scoop it with tortilla chips, roll it into a burrito, or even slurp it straight. After all, nothing beats a tasty guacamole!

Little Red Hen and her friends enjoy guacamole in this made-up story, but in real life, animals shouldn't eat avocados, so please don't feed them to your pets. That means more guacamole for you!

GLOSSARY

ahuacamolli The original Aztec name for guacamole that comes from the words ahuacati (avocado) and mulli (sauce) in the language of the Aztecs.

armadillo This mammal's name is Spanish for "little armored one"; its body is covered in an armor of bony plates and leathery skin. The nine-banded armadillo that lives in the Mexican forest eats insects and is a great digger. It digs burrows to nest in. While gathering nesting materials like leaves and twigs, it hops on its hind legs. When startled, nine-banded armadillos can jump four feet straight upward!

avocado A pear-shaped fruit with leather-like skin and soft, light green flesh that grows on trees native to Mexico and Central America.

burrito A Mexican dish in which a tortilla is rolled around a filling, usually beans or meat and cheese.

casa Spanish for "house."

cilantro An herb whose leaves are used in Mexican cooking.

coati The white-nosed coati, or coatimundi, lives in the forests of Mexico. This mammal has a long, ringed tail and can reach the size of a house cat. It eats insects, fruit, eggs, and small animals. It climbs trees easily, where it sleeps at night.

cocina Spanish for "kitchen."

cumin A spice used in Mexican cooking.

gallinita Spanish for "little hen."

guacamole A blend of mashed avocado, vegetables, and seasonings that's believed to have originated with the Aztec people of Mexico in the 1300s.

iguana These large lizards are right at home on the ground or up in the treetops of the Mexican forest. Because they are cold-blooded, they like to bask in the sun to maintain their correct body temperature. They eat fruit and leafy plants. Their green and brown coloring provides good camouflage, helping them blend in with their surroundings so predators can't see them.

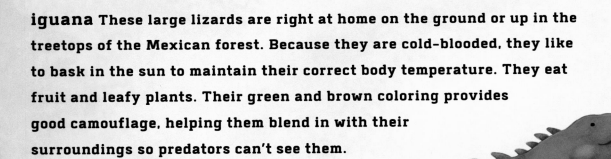

masa A corn-flour dough used to make tortillas and other Mexican foods.

molcajete Made of lava stone, the traditional mortar and pestle used in Mexico to mash and mix guacamole. Guacamole is often served right from the molcajete.

queso Spanish for "cheese."

roja Spanish for "red."

taco A Mexican dish in which a tortilla is folded and stuffed with a filling, often beans, meat, and cheese.

tortilla A soft, thin Mexican flatbread made from corn or wheat flour.

For the ahuacamolli fans—S.W.

To my parents, who taught me to make great guacamole—L.G.

STERLING CHILDREN'S BOOKS
New York

An Imprint of Sterling Publishing Co., Inc.
1166 Avenue of the Americas
New York, NY 10036

ISBN 978-1-4549-2253-7

Distributed in Canada by Sterling Publishing Co., Inc.
c/o Canadian Manda Group, 664 Annette Street
Toronto, Ontario M6S 2C8, Canada
Distributed in the United Kingdom by GMC Distribution Services
Castle Place, 166 High Street, Lewes, East Sussex BN7 1XU, England
Distributed in Australia by NewSouth Books
University of New South Wales, Sydney, NSW 2052, Australia

For information about custom editions, special sales, and premium and corporate purchases, please
contact Sterling Special Sales at 800-805-5489 or specialsales@sterlingpublishing.com.

Manufactured in China

Lot #:
2 4 6 8 10 9 7 5 3 1
12/18

sterlingpublishing.com

Jacket and interior design by Ryan Thomann

5